1299

J F DRI

P9-ARC-457

Driscoll, Laura.

WITHDRAWN

Dora helps Diego!

Dora Helps Diego!

by Laura Driscoll
illustrated by Tom Mangano

Ready-to-Read

Simon Spotlight/Nick Jr.
New York   London   Toronto   Sydney

Based on the TV series *Dora the Explorer*® as seen on Nick Jr.®

SIMON SPOTLIGHT
An imprint of Simon & Schuster Children's Publishing Division
1230 Avenue of the Americas, New York, New York 10020
© 2007 Viacom International Inc. All rights reserved.
NICK JR., *Dora the Explorer*, and all related titles, logos, and characters are
registered trademarks of Viacom International Inc.
SIMON SPOTLIGHT, READY-TO-READ, and colophon are registered trademarks of Simon & Schuster,
Manufactured in the United States of America
4 6 8 10 9 7 5

Library of Congress Cataloging-in-Publication Data
Driscoll, Laura.
Dora helps Diego! / by Laura Driscoll ; illustrated by Tom Mangano.
—1st ed.
p. cm. — (Dora the explorer) (Ready-to-read)
ISBN-13: 978-1-4169-1509-6 (pbk.)
ISBN-10: 1-4169-1509-5 (pbk.)
I. Mangano, Tom. II. Dora the explorer (Television program)
III. Title. IV. Series. V. Series: Ready-to-read.
PZ7.D79Dor 2007
2006009688

Hi! I am  .
DORA

, , and I

need your help!

Oh, no! is missing!

BABY JAGUAR

 cannot find him!

DIEGO

 and I

BOOTS

are helping find him.

DIEGO

Will you help too?

Great!

Help us find  !

BABY JAGUAR

Look up in that .

TREE

I see a .

TAIL

BABY JAGUAR has a **TAIL** .

Does it belong to ? **BABY JAGUAR**

No.

It is a  SNAKE getting out of the  SUN .

Where is  ?
BABY JAGUAR

Look behind those .

FLOWERS

I see .

FEET

has .

BABY JAGUAR   FEET

Do they belong to ?

BABY JAGUAR

No.

It is
ISA

working in her .
GARDEN

Where is  ?

BABY JAGUAR

Look behind that trunk.

TREE

I see .

WHISKERS

 has .

BABY JAGUAR WHISKERS

Do those belong

WHISKERS

to ?

BABY JAGUAR

No.

It is  SWIPER, that sneaky fox.

Where is  ?
BABY JAGUAR

Look behind the .

SLIDE

I see ⬤.

SPOTS

BABY JAGUAR has SPOTS.

Do they belong to BABY JAGUAR?

No.

It is the scarf that

belongs to BENNY.

Will we **ever** find BABY JAGUAR ?

We need to go back to the Animal Rescue Center.

We open the .

DOOR

We cannot believe it!

We see a ,

TAIL   FEET

, and .

WHISKERS   SPOTS

Here is !

BABY JAGUAR

 is so happy!

DIEGO

We found !

BABY JAGUAR

Thanks for helping!